MOLLY PITCHER

MOLLY PITCHER

Jan Gleiter and Kathleen Thompson

Illustrated by Charles Shaw

Ideals Publishing Corporation
Nashville, Tennessee

It was June 28, 1778, and the American soldiers were on the move. They marched forward in the blazing sun. They were a ragged bunch. Some were barefoot. All were dusty and hot. Here and there,

trees cast shade. But the soldiers did not stop. On they went, toward Monmouth, toward the British. The march did not seem fast enough to be a chase. But it was.

The British soldiers were resting at Monmouth on their way to New York. They had spent an easy winter in Philadelphia. They had slept in snug, warm houses. They had eaten good meals. They had listened to music and danced. And they had laughed at the American rebels who dared to make war against them.

The Americans had spent the winter camped at
Valley Forge, Pennsylvania. They had slept in
log cabins through which the wind had whistled.
They had wrapped rags around their feet when their
shoes wore out. They had eaten flat cakes made from
flour and water.

The ones who stayed were the tough ones. They
had used that long, cold winter. They hadn't listened
to music. They had listened to orders. They hadn't
danced. They had marched. And when the winter
ended, they had a new spirit. They were a real army.
Now their orders were to march to the town of
Monmouth, in New Jersey—to catch the British and
to fight them. So onward they went.

9

The sun beat down on the marching men. It was one of the hottest days of that summer. A woman marched with the men. Her name was Mary Hays, but her husband and friends called her Molly.

Molly Hays was frightened. Mostly she was frightened for her husband, John. John was a gunner. It was his job to fire one of the huge cannons

that were pulled from battle to battle. It was a
dangerous job. The enemy always tried to stop the
cannons, any way they could.

But Molly was proud, too. She was proud of John.
She was proud of the rebels. She was proud of their
leader, General George Washington.

Molly knew General Washington. She knew the kind of man he was. He had been the soldiers' leader during the freezing months at Valley Forge. Washington had suffered along with his men, sharing whatever he had with those who had less. He had kept the soldiers from giving up. He had made them proud, like he was. Molly knew. She had been there too, cooking and washing and doing what had to be done.

Molly had seen how Washington's men trusted him. She did, too. But she knew that there would be a battle today. And she was frightened.

Suddenly, above the noise of marching feet, Molly heard shouts. Something was wrong. Soldiers were coming from up ahead, coming fast. They were Americans. These were the men that Washington had sent out earlier to attack part of the British army. They should be miles away, fighting. But they were retreating, moving back towards Washington and the rest of his men.

15

General Washington was furious. His soldiers had retreated and ruined his plan. He knew it wasn't the men's fault. But his voice was cold as he spoke with the general he had sent to lead them. Now he would have to make a new plan, and there was no time to lose.

Washington thought fast. That was part of what made him a great general. He seemed to be able to read the enemy's mind. He shouted orders, new orders. His officers nodded and ran to tell their men.

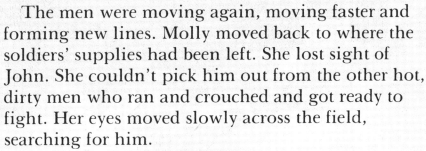

The men were moving again, moving faster and forming new lines. Molly moved back to where the soldiers' supplies had been left. She lost sight of John. She couldn't pick him out from the other hot, dirty men who ran and crouched and got ready to fight. Her eyes moved slowly across the field, searching for him.

And then the air was filled with the noise of cannons and muskets and rifles. The Battle of Monmouth had begun.

In between the sounds of battle, Molly could hear cries. "Water! Water!" Men were falling, falling from the heat.

Molly wasn't a gunner. She wasn't a soldier of any kind. But she was as brave as any of them, and she knew when she was needed.

Picking up her long skirts, she ran. She grabbed up a pitcher and raced through the trees to a spring. She filled the pitcher with cold, clear water and hurried back toward the fighting.

Molly ran out onto the battlefield. The air was thick with the smell of gunpowder. A musket ball whizzed past her ear. But all she heard was the cry for water.

A soldier kneeled in the dirt, pouring gunpowder into his musket. His hair stuck to his forehead, and his throat was dry with dust. Suddenly a woman knelt beside him. She held a pitcher of cool water to his lips. He drank deeply, looking into the steady eyes so close to his own. And then, before he could even thank her, she was gone. He watched her move ahead, crouching and running to another thirsty soldier, and another.

Molly moved quickly. She could tell at a glance which men were most in need, and she went to them first. Through the clouds of dust, she looked for John. Where was he? But she had a job to do. And, worried as she was about her husband, she could not stop to search for him.

Time and again, she ran back to the spring. The safety of the trees called to her. She needed to stop. She needed to be safe for awhile. But she could not, not while American soldiers were fighting for American freedom. Not while American men needed the bravery of an American woman.

Molly Hays had been born in America, near
Trenton, New Jersey. She had grown up listening to
people talk about having to obey British laws
without having any say in what laws were made. She
heard what the people called patriots were saying. It
made sense to her. It made sense that people should
have rights. It made sense that people should not
have to obey the laws of another nation, far away.

In the years before her marriage, Molly had worked
as a servant. She was a hard worker, and a cheerful
one. When she was fifteen, she married John Hays, a
young barber. He lived in the same Pennsylvania
town she worked in then. John felt the same way
about freedom that Molly did. So, when the war
began, he joined the army.

But John and Molly did not let the war keep them
apart. Many American women went with their
husbands from camp to camp. They would rather be

cold and hungry in an army camp than sitting in
front of a fire in a cozy house, waiting and
wondering and doing nothing. Molly Hays was one
of those women.

Like the others, Molly had many jobs in the camps.
The things she had learned as a servant were useful
to her during the war. She didn't mind hard work.
She didn't mind being uncomfortable. And she
wanted to be part of the fight for freedom.

Now, at the Battle of Monmouth, Molly was more a part of the fight than she had ever been before. Once, a cannonball slammed into a wagon. A flying piece of broken wood knocked her to the ground. Jumping to her feet, she snatched up the pitcher. She hardly noticed the fall except that it had spilled her precious water. She raced, again, for the spring.

This time, on her way back through the battlefield, she saw a familiar back. She could always recognize John, even when she couldn't see his face. There was

something about the proud way he held his shoulders. But now he was sagging from exhaustion, hanging over the cannon. And, as Molly ran to his side, she saw him fall.

Her heart leaped with fright. But when she reached him and knelt over him, she could see he was not wounded. He was overcome by the heat of the sun. Molly soaked a rag with cool water from her pitcher and tied it around his head.

Quickly and gently, Molly moved John so that his head was in a small pool of shade made by the cannon. Then she snatched up the ramrod that John had dropped when he fell. The cannon must be fired! It must not stop firing for any longer than it took to load a new cannonball. Not even one cannon could be silent.

"Load!" she shouted to a soldier behind the big gun. Then she slammed the ramrod down the barrel of the cannon to pound the gunpowder down so it

could fire the solid iron ball.

The huge gun sounded, and sounded again.

It took every bit of Molly's strength to shove the ramrod down the barrel, time and again. Every time she did it, she knew that if a ball jammed, it would make the cannon itself explode. But on she went, coughing from the gases that poured from the barrel when a ball was fired, burning her hands on the hot metal.

The sun that had blazed so fiercely all day sank slowly in the sky. The battle went on, and on. But, finally, darkness did what the British had been unable to do. The darkness silenced the guns. The Battle of Monmouth was over.

Molly sank to the ground, too tired to move. She could hear soldiers stumbling past. But then the footsteps stopped.

"It's Molly!" said a voice. "Molly Hays!"
"No," said another voice. "That's Molly Pitcher!"
A cry went up. "Molly Pitcher!"
The grateful soldiers lifted her gently. They carried her and John from the field. They laid them down on a bed of blankets and washed the dust from their faces.

And then, in the darkness, everyone rested. Everyone except the British. In the cover of night, the British slipped away.

Ten thousand men had fought on each side. Sixty-nine Americans had died. More than three times as many British were buried on the battlefield. The loss of lives was sad and terrible. But it could have been worse. It surely would have been worse, at least for the Americans, without the courage of a twenty-four-year-old woman—a woman known to this day as Molly Pitcher.